Brooke
the Photographer
Fairy

To Hannah with love

Special thanks to Rachel Elliot

No part of this publication may be reproduced, stored in a retrieval
system, or transmitted in any form or by any means, electronic,
mechanical, photocopying, recording, or otherwise, without written
permission of the publisher. For information regarding permission,
write to Rainbow Magic Limited c/o HIT Entertainment,
830 South Greenville Avenue, Allen, TX 75002-3320.

ISBN 978-0-545-48489-3

12 11 10 9 8 7 6 5 4 3 2 1   13 14 15 16 17 18/0

Printed in the U.S.A.   40

This edition first printing, July 2013

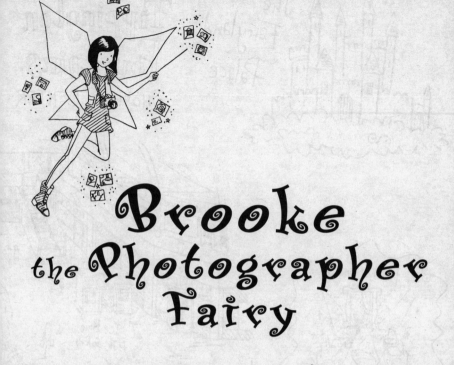

Brooke
the Photographer
Fairy

by Daisy Meadows

SCHOLASTIC INC.

I'm the king of designer fashion,
Looking stylish is my passion.
Ice Blue's the name of my fashion line,
The designs are fabulous and they're all mine!

Some people think my clothes are odd,
But I will get the fashion world's nod.
Fashion Fairy magic will make my dream come true —
Soon everyone will wear Ice Blue!

Contents

Photo Fiasco   1

Flashes on the Roof   13

Jack Frost, Supermodel!   23

Toy-store Trouble   33

Snapping on Ice!   45

Surprise Shower!   57

Photo Fiasco

"This place is so beautiful," said Kirsty Tate, gazing around at the lush green grass, the bright flowers, and the potted palms. "Isn't it funny seeing a garden up so high?"

She was standing in the middle of the roof garden on top of the brand-new Tippington Fountains Shopping Center.

The glass-fronted Roof Garden Café was at the far end. Next to the café was a glass elevator that took visitors down to the mall.

"It must be even prettier when the sun's shining," replied her best friend, Rachel Walker. "All the glass must really sparkle."

They both looked up at the gray rain clouds that were gathering overhead.

"Yes, it's too bad that it isn't a sunny day," Kirsty agreed.

All week long, the girls had been involved in the design competition at

the new shopping mall. There was a
fashion show planned for the next day to
celebrate the end of the
mall's first week.

"I think this is
the best place
to have a
photo shoot,
even if the
weather isn't
perfect," said

Rachel with a smile.

Kirsty's and Rachel's outfits had
been among those chosen to be in the
fashion show. Today, the winners were
taking part in a photo shoot for *The
Fountains Fashion News* magazine.
Supermodel Jessica Jarvis and designer
Ella McCauley were there, too. They

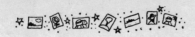

had been special guests at the shopping mall all week, and now they were helping the kids make sure that their colorful, imaginative clothes looked as good as possible. Kirsty was wearing the dress that she had made out of scarves, and Rachel had put on her rainbow-painted jeans.

Cam Carson, the photographer, was busy organizing the winners into groups. "I'd like you all to choose themes for your photos," she said. "It should be something that connects with your designs and means something special to you."

4

Kirsty turned to Rachel.

"What should we pick?" she asked. "What fits with rainbow colors?"

"Easy," said Rachel. "Our theme should be friendship. That fits with rainbows — the fairies taught us that!"

The girls grabbed hands and smiled at each other.

"That's perfect," Kirsty replied. "We're really lucky. I'm so glad we met each other that day on the boat to Rainspell Island."

"Me, too," said Rachel.

Ever since that vacation on Rainspell Island, the girls had shared a wonderful secret. They were friends with the fairies! They often traveled to Fairyland and helped outwit Jack Frost and his goblins. Their friendship had grown stronger and stronger with every adventure they shared.

The other competition winners were getting ready for their photograph to be taken, too. A boy named Dean was wearing a space-themed T-shirt and carrying a model spaceship. A girl named Layla had designed a soccer uniform and

had a soccer ball tucked
under her arm.

"You all look
wonderful," said Jessica.
"Now remember, the best
photographs are taken
when you look happy
and natural. So just try
to relax and smile!"

Cam Carson picked up
her camera and tucked her
brown hair behind her ears.

"OK, I'm ready," she said. "Who's
going first?"

"Rachel and Kirsty are first on the
list," said Ella, ushering them forward.

The girls put their arms around each
other and smiled. But just as Cam took

the photograph, Kirsty's hair blew in
front of her face.

"Oops," said Cam with a laugh. "Let's
try again."

She pressed the button once more and
then checked the picture on the screen.

"Oh, no, you were blinking," she said
to Rachel. "Third time's a charm!"

She pressed the button again, but this time her finger was in front of the lens.

"What's the matter with me today?" she muttered.

There was a low rumble of thunder, and everyone looked up. The dark rain clouds were moving closer.

"I'll have to use the flash," said Cam, changing the settings on her camera.

Before she could take another photo, there was a bright flash from the camera.

"Now it's going off by itself!" she said, sounding annoyed. "Just a minute, everyone.

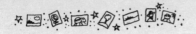

My camera just doesn't seem to want to
work today!"

She fiddled with the controls again, but
before she could press the button there
was another unexpected flash. Taken by
surprise, Layla dropped her soccer ball
and it bounced toward the edge of the
roof. Dean tried to catch it and skidded
to a stop right near the
edge. He lost his grip
on his model
spaceship.
It crashed
to the
floor and
broke
into three
pieces!

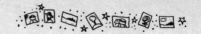

"It's not our lucky day." Cam sighed as Dean picked up the pieces of his spaceship.

"This is no ordinary bad luck," Rachel whispered to Kirsty, looking worried. "This is the work of Jack Frost!"

Flashes on the Roof

Kirsty nodded, thinking about everything that had happened that week. It had all started on the first day of fall break. The girls had been whisked off to Fairyland to see their friends in a fashion show. But Jack Frost and the goblins also showed up, modeling crazy bright-blue outfits from Jack Frost's designer label, Ice Blue.

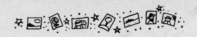

To everyone's horror, Jack Frost had announced that everyone would soon be wearing Ice Blue clothes — designed by him! With a bolt of icy magic, he stole the magical objects belonging to the Fashion Fairies and carried them off to Tippington Fountains Shopping Center.

Without their magic objects, the Fashion Fairies couldn't take good care of fashion in the human and fairy worlds. The girls knew that they had to do something. They had already helped five of the fairies get their magic objects back — but there were still two more to find.

Kirsty's thoughts were interrupted by a drop of rain falling onto the tip of her nose.

Cam sighed as she looked up at the gray clouds.

"Nothing's going right today," she said. "OK, everyone, let's take a break and go inside. Maybe it's just going to be a passing shower."

She sheltered her camera equipment under a large umbrella, and then followed Jessica, Ella, and the kids into the Roof Garden Café. Kirsty and Rachel stayed back and exchanged a secret glance.

"This *has* to have something to do with Jack Frost," said Rachel.

"Yes, and his awful goblins," Kirsty agreed. "The weather forecast didn't say anything about rain. It was supposed to be sunny."

"Come on, let's go inside before we get wet," said Kirsty.

They turned toward the café, but then Rachel grabbed her friend's arm in excitement. She had seen something out of the corner of her eye. "Kirsty, look," she said, pointing at Cam's equipment.

The camera was perched on top of a tripod, and the flash seemed to be glowing brighter than usual. It was hard to see the camera behind the golden glow.

"Why do you think Cam didn't turn off the flash? She isn't using it," said Kirsty.

"That's not a flash," said Rachel, looking at the glowing light more closely. "It's Brooke the Photographer Fairy!"

Brooke smiled and waved at them.

The girls glanced back at the café to make sure no one was watching, and then they hurried over to the little fairy. She wore skinny jeans and a tunic top, and her glossy black hair seemed to swing as she hovered in front of them. Her dark eyes glinted with fun and excitement.

"Hello, Kirsty! Hello, Rachel! Did I interrupt a photo shoot? You both look fabulous!" she said.

"Thanks," said Kirsty with a smile. "But it was the rain that interrupted the photo shoot, not you. Everything seems to be going wrong for the photographer today."

"That's why I'm here," said Brooke. "While my magic camera is missing, all fashion shoots will be ruined. I was hoping that you'd help me, just like you've helped the other Fashion Fairies."

"Of course we will," said Rachel eagerly. "We'll do everything we can to find your magic camera."

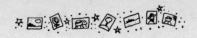

Kirsty was staring over at the other side of the roof garden. "There's something going on over there," Kirsty said. "I keep seeing lots of flashes."

"Like camera flashes?" asked Brooke.

"Yes," said Kirsty. "Look, there's another one!"

Rachel and Brooke saw a bright flash.

"That's strange," said Rachel. "Cam's supposed to be the only photographer up here this morning."

"Let's go and investigate," Brooke suggested. "I have a feeling that something funny is going on over there."

"But remember, no one can see you," said Kirsty. "There are lots of people in the café over there. One of them might spot you!"

"Here, hide in my bag," Rachel said,

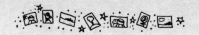

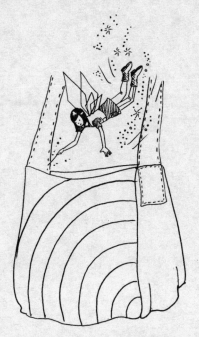

holding open her pretty rainbow-colored purse. Brooke fluttered into Rachel's bag, and then the girls hurried over to the far side of the roof garden. There were even more flashes coming from that direction now, and they could hear giggles and squawks. What was going on?

Jack Frost, Supermodel!!

The girls crouched down behind a row of large potted palm trees and cautiously peeked around the green leaves. In the middle of a small clearing, Jack Frost and four goblins were having their own photo shoot!

Jack Frost was wearing an Ice Blue jumpsuit, with bell-bottoms and a long,

rounded collar. He had completed his
outfit with a sequinned
electric-blue cape
and a matching top
hat. He was posing
with one hand on
his hip and the
other pointing up
to the gloomy sky.
He looked very
pleased with himself!
"You!" he bellowed
at the shortest goblin.
"Fluff up my beard!"

As the little goblin rushed forward to
obey, Jack jabbed his bony finger into the
squashy stomach of a plump goblin.

"You! Get me a different hat!" he
demanded. "I want the glittery cowboy

hat, and I want
it NOW!"

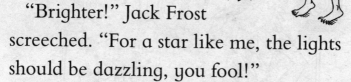

A third goblin
was busily shining
electric lights on
Jack Frost from all
angles.

"Brighter!" Jack Frost
screeched. "For a star like me, the lights
should be dazzling, you fool!"

As the lights grew even brighter, the
drizzle stopped and a ray of sunshine
fell across Jack Frost's face. The plump
goblin handed him the cowboy hat. A
skinny goblin held up a little camera
and called out instructions to the cranky
model.

"That's great!" he yelled as Jack Frost
gave him a fake, forced smile. "Let's see

those pearly white teeth! Give me attitude!
Give me pizzazz! Who's the boss?"

"ME!" Jack Frost exclaimed, giving a
huge grin and raising one eyebrow.

The photographer snapped away as

Jack Frost struck pose after pose. Brooke
peeked out of Rachel's bag and gasped.
Then she fluttered up to Rachel's

shoulder and folded
her arms across her
chest.

"That's my
magic camera,"
she said. "I'm
so glad we
found it, but
I'm very angry
with Jack Frost

and the goblins for stealing it!"

"We have to get it back quickly," said
Rachel in a determined voice. "The
goblins don't know how to take good
care of things, and it would be horrible if
they broke the camera."

At that moment, the skinny goblin
nearly dropped the camera! Brooke
almost squealed out loud, but the goblin

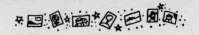

caught it just in time.
He put the strap
around his neck.

"That was close,"
said Kirsty. "We'd
better do something
fast, and I think I
have an idea. Brooke,
can you disguise me and
Rachel as photographers? Maybe we
can get close enough to the magic
camera to get it back."

"No problem," said Brooke with a wink.
She waved her wand, and a fountain
of silver fairy sparkles fell over the girls.
A big camera appeared on a strap
around Kirsty's neck, and Rachel found
herself carrying spare lenses, a tripod,

and a couple of handheld lights. Their
beautiful clothes disappeared and were
replaced with bright
blue suits that
looked like they
might be from
Jack Frost's Ice
Blue designer
label.

Brooke hid
in the pocket of
Rachel's jacket.
Then the girls took
deep breaths and stepped out from
behind the potted palms. They walked
slowly toward the little group.

Jack Frost started shouting as soon as
he saw them.

"Clear out!" he hollered. "This is a very important photo shoot and you're getting in the way. GET LOST!"

The girls ignored his rudeness and smiled at him.

"We're so sorry," said Kirsty. "It's just that we work for *Fashion World* magazine, and we're HUGE fans of your Ice Blue fashion label. We're here to take

your photo for the cover of the next issue."

"But we can see you're busy, so we'll leave," Rachel added, turning away.

"WAIT!" shouted Jack Frost. "I

want to be a cover model! Come back
here, NOW!"

Kirsty and Rachel stopped, and Jack
Frost started barking orders at his goblins.

"Make my hair look more pointy!
Brush my coat! Polish my shoes!
HURRY UP!"

The goblins scurried around their boss,
yelping and squealing as they tried to
follow all his instructions at once. The
smallest goblin held up a mirror, and
Jack Frost nodded, primping himself.

"Are you ready?" asked Kirsty, holding
up her camera. She just hoped that her
plan would work!

Toy-store Trouble

"This will be the most important photo of my life," said Jack Frost. "How do I look?"

"You look very handsome, Your Iciness," said the plump goblin.

"Then I'm ready!" said Jack Frost.

Kirsty pressed the button to take a photo, but nothing happened.

"Oh, no. I think
the battery must be
dead." She groaned.
"I don't have an
extra! What am I
going to do?"
"We'll just have
to try again later.
We can use it in
next month's issue,"
said Rachel.

"I'm NOT waiting!" Jack Frost shouted.
"Do something!"

Rachel hid a smile. She had guessed
that Jack Frost wouldn't have the patience
to wait.

"Well, there is one thing we could do,"
said Kirsty, trying to sound like she had
just had the idea. "If your photographer

would lend us
his camera,
we could take
your picture
with that."

The skinny
goblin clutched
the camera to
his chest. Jack
Frost turned to him
and narrowed his cold eyes.

"Hand it over," he snapped.

"But — but — but you said . . ." the
goblin protested.

"NOW!" roared Jack Frost.

With a jump of fright, the goblin held
out the precious magic camera. Kirsty
and Rachel exchanged a glance — their
plan was working! Kirsty stretched out

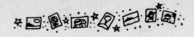

her hand, her fingers brushing the strap of the camera. . . .

Inside Rachel's pocket, Brooke was very excited to hear that the girls were going to get the camera. She couldn't resist peeking out to see what was happening.

"STOP!" bellowed Jack Frost.

Kirsty froze, and the goblin snatched the camera back. Jack Frost had seen Brooke in Rachel's jacket pocket!

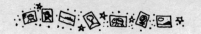

Jack Frost sent a bolt of icy magic
toward the girls, and the camera flew
out of the goblin's hand and into Jack's
grabby fingers. Two more ice bolts sent
Kirsty and Rachel
tumbling to the
ground, and
then Jack
Frost ran
past them,
toward
the glass
elevator.
The goblins
followed as fast as
they could, and they dove into the
elevator at once. It was a tight squeeze,
but they all fit in, and the doors started
to close.

"Quick, stop them!" cried Rachel, scrambling to her feet and racing after the pesky crew.

But as she reached the elevator, the doors slid shut and the goblins and Jack Frost were carried downward. The last thing Rachel saw before the elevator disappeared was four goblin faces pressed up against the glass, all sticking their tongues out at her.

"Oh, no. We lost them!" Kirsty exclaimed, running up behind Rachel.

"We have to follow them!" cried Rachel.

"We'll be quicker if you can both fly," said Brooke.

She glanced around to make sure no one from the café could see them. Then she zoomed into the air above the girls and waved her wand in a wide circle. Silver fairy dust sprinkled down on Rachel and Kirsty.

In a flash, the girls were swept off

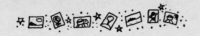

their feet and into the air. Sparkling
fairy dust swirled all around them,

shrinking them
until they were
the same size
as Brooke.
Delicate
wings
fluttered on
their backs,
and the girls
hovered beside

Brooke and smiled at each other.

"Ready?" Brooke asked.

"Ready!" said Kirsty and Rachel
together.

"Let's go!" Brooke cried, swooping
down the staircase.

A few seconds later, the three fairies

zipped out of
the stairwell
and into the
mall. They
flew as
close to the
ceiling as
they could, so
the crowd of
shoppers wouldn't see them. The mall
was busier than ever.

"I hope we're going to be able to spot
Jack Frost and the goblins among all
these people," said Kirsty.

"Look down there," said Rachel,
pointing down to the Winter Woolies
booth.

One of the displays had been knocked
over, and shoppers were getting tangled

up in the long woolen scarves on the
floor. Shoppers were stumbling around,
bumping into one another.

"If we look for trouble, I bet Jack Frost
won't be far away," Rachel continued.

"Look!" said Kirsty suddenly. "Someone

dressed in bright blue just ran into
Tippington Toys. Let's go and see if it
was Jack Frost!"

They all zoomed down to the toy store
and swooped over a group of kids. At the

far end of the store, another group of kids
was standing around a rocking horse.
They had all put on funny hats and
clothes from the dress-up section, but
something about the way they were
standing made Brooke want to look
closer.

"They don't look like ordinary kids,"
said the little fairy.

As they neared the group, they saw
long green noses sticking out from under
the hats, and bony green fingers reaching
out to stroke the rocking horse's mane.

"They're goblins!" cried Rachel.

Snapping on Ice!

It didn't take long for the girls to realize
that it was Jack Frost on the rocking horse.

"Take those horrible clothes off," he
snapped at the goblins. "They're not
made by Ice Blue, and that means they're
GARBAGE."

Grumbling, the goblins pulled off
their dress-up clothes. Then one of them

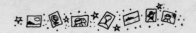

grabbed a scooter from a nearby display.
The other three did the same, and they
all started to scoot around the store at
top speed.

Brooke, Rachel, and Kirsty perched on
a red kite that was hanging from the
ceiling and looked down at the chaos
the goblins were causing below. They
rolled their scooters over the feet of other
shoppers, knocked over displays, and
made a terrible racket.

"Look at Jack Frost!" shouted Kirsty over all the noise.

He was sitting in front of a toy makeup table, playing with his hair and taking photographs of himself with Brooke's magic camera.

"He's keeping a tight grip on my camera," said Brooke with a sigh. "How are we going to get it back?"

Rachel spotted a playhouse in the corner of the store and gasped.

"I think I have an idea," she said. "Hold on to the kite and flap your wings as hard as you can!"

Kirsty and Brooke started to flap their wings, and they felt the kite start to move beneath them, tugging on the string that tied it to the ceiling.

"We need to make it fly toward Jack Frost," said Rachel in a breathless voice. "Flap harder!"

"I can't," groaned Kirsty.

"Maybe my magic can help," said
Brooke. She tapped her wand on the kite
and it started to move.

"Steer it toward Jack Frost!" Rachel
cried. "Try to chase him into the
playhouse."

The kite picked up speed as the friends
steered it toward Jack Frost.

"What?" Jack Frost exclaimed as he saw
the kite coming straight toward him. He
ran away and ducked into the playhouse,
with Brooke and the girls right behind.
He was trapped!

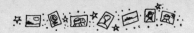

The three fairies hovered in the doorway.

"You're cornered," said Kirsty. "Just give the camera back and we'll let you go."

"No way," said Jack Frost, hiding it behind him. "This takes great photos of me, and I'm keeping it. Goblins, get over here now!"

The girls heard the sound of four scooters being dropped on the floor,

followed by four pairs of feet thumping toward the playhouse. The goblins peeked through the window, and then Jack Frost flicked his wand. There was a loud crack and a flash of blue magic.

"To my Ice Castle!" shouted Jack Frost. A second later, he and his goblins had disappeared.

"We have to follow them, or I'll never get my camera back," said Brooke. "Girls, will you come to the Ice Castle with me?"

"Of course!" said Rachel. Kirsty nodded in agreement.

Brooke waved her wand and said a quick spell:

"To Jack Frost's home of ice and snow,
In an instant we must go.
Let us follow where
they flew,
But keep us
safely out
of view!"

There was a bright golden flash, and then the girls found themselves sitting on a frosty tree branch in the garden of Jack Frost's castle.

"Look down
there," said
Kirsty
quietly.
She
pointed to
a clearing
among snow-
covered trees. Jack
Frost and the four goblins
were standing around a large
pond that had a waterfall pouring into it
from a high rocky cliff.

"This is a much better setting for my
photo shoot," Jack Frost was saying. "All
it needs is a little extra frostiness!"

He raised his wand and *zap!* The pond
froze over. *Zap!* Ice sculptures appeared
around the pond, wearing Ice Blue

designs. *Zap!* The waterfall froze to create a giant sheet of ice, like a mirror.

"What a wonderful sight," said Jack Frost, gazing at his reflection.

He took a few photos of himself with the magic camera, which he didn't seem willing to return to the goblin photographer. Then he looked around.

"These trees aren't icy enough," he grumbled.

Zap! Zap! Zap! Tree after tree was suddenly weighed down with thick, sharp icicles.

"He's turning this way!" cried Brooke. "Duck!"

The three fairies zoomed out of the way as the tree they were sitting in was decorated with icicles. When he saw them, Jack Frost gave a yell of fury.

"What are you pesky fairies doing here?" he bellowed. "You're trying to ruin my photo shoot! I'll make you sorry you ever THOUGHT of coming here!"

Surprise Shower!

The fairies flew left and right, trying to dart out of the way as Jack Frost tried to zap them with his wand. The sculptures cracked and exploded as the ice bolts struck them. Icicles plunged to the ground. The goblins had to dive out of the way to avoid being hit!

"Kirsty! Brooke!" Rachel shouted over

the yelps and squeals
of the goblins.
"Meet me at the
waterfall!"

The three
fairies zoomed
toward the frozen
waterfall and
zipped behind it, hidden from Jack Frost
for a moment.

"Do you have a plan?" Kirsty panted.

Rachel nodded and hurriedly started to
whisper to the others.

"Come out from behind my waterfall!"
Jack Frost screeched. "I'll turn you all
into ice sculptures!"

Rachel peeked around the side of the
waterfall.

"He's pretty close," she whispered. *"Now!"*

Brooke waved her wand, and the frozen waterfall melted. Brooke's magic sent a shower of icy water gushing down on top of Jack Frost!

"YOWWEEEEEE!" he screamed.

In shock, he dropped the camera, and Kirsty swooped down, catching it just before it hit the ground. Rachel followed her, and together they managed to lift the camera up to where Brooke was hovering. As soon as Brooke touched it, the camera shrank

back to its normal
fairy size.
Dripping wet
and furious, Jack
Frost shook his fist at
the three fairies, who were
fluttering just out of his reach.

"You haven't won!" he raged. "I still
have one of your precious magical
objects, and as long as I have that, I can
ruin things in the fashion world!"

"We're not going to let you do that!"
said Rachel.

Before Jack Frost could think of a
reply, Brooke waved her wand and
a stream of fairy dust swirled around
the three fairies. When it disappeared,
they found themselves in the roof garden
of the shopping mall once again.

The rain had stopped and the sun was coming out from behind the clouds. Kirsty and Rachel followed Brooke behind some tall, leafy plants, where they were out of sight.

"I'd better change you back to normal," said Brooke. "Now that the sun has come out, your photo shoot can go ahead. Besides, I have to return to Fairyland and tell the other Fashion Fairies about our adventure!"

She waved her wand and turned Rachel and Kirsty back to their usual size. Their Ice Blue suits had disappeared, and they were wearing their own colorful designs again.

"Good-bye," said
Brooke, fluttering
in front of them.
"And thank you
both — I'm so
happy to have my
magic camera back
at last."

"We loved helping
you," Kirsty replied.
"Good-bye, Brooke!"

Brooke waved and twirled upward,
faster and faster, until she was just a
golden blur. She vanished in a flutter of
wings, leaving behind a dazzling spray
of fairy dust that shimmered like a
fireworks display.

"Rachel! Kirsty!" called Jessica, making
them jump.

The girls stepped out from behind the plants and saw Jessica, Cam, Ella, and the other winners standing outside the café. Dean had fixed his spaceship, and Layla had her soccer ball back.

"Ready to give the photo shoot another try?" asked Cam.

Everyone nodded, and Cam asked Dean and Layla to pose first. This time, the camera worked perfectly, and nothing else went wrong.

"Fantastic!" exclaimed Cam, snapping shot after shot. "Wonderful! These look great!"

When it was Rachel and Kirsty's turn, they posed in front of the potted palms with their arms around each other. Just  as Cam was about to take the picture, something wonderful happened — a rainbow appeared in the sky behind the girls!

"What an amazing natural backdrop for the shot!" exclaimed Cam. "These photos are going to be perfect for the special issue of *The Fountains Fashion News.*"

"I can't wait for the fashion show!" said Ella. "Looking at all of you, I can

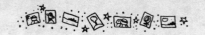

tell that it's going to be absolutely
fantastic."

Kirsty, Rachel, Dean, and Layla
smiled at one another.

"It'll be awesome," said Dean.

"Tomorrow is going to be so much
fun," added Layla.

Rachel and Kirsty hoped that they
were right. But there was still one more
magical object to get back from Jack
Frost! A worried frown appeared on
Kirsty's face as she thought about it.
Rachel grinned at her best friend and
squeezed her hand.

"We won't let Jack Frost ruin the
fashion show," she whispered. "Don't
worry, Kirsty. The Fashion Fairies can
count on us!"

RAINBOW magic™

THE FASHION FAIRIES

Kirsty and Rachel helped Brooke
find her magic camera.
Now it's time for the girls to help

Lola
the Fashion Show Fairy!

Read on for a sneak peek. . . .

Off to the Show

Kirsty Tate was *very* excited. Today, she and her best friend, Rachel Walker, were going to be in a fashion show! Not only that, but they would be wearing outfits they had designed and made themselves, after entering a special competition held at Tippington Fountains Shopping Center earlier that week.

"I hope I don't trip on the catwalk."

Rachel giggled as she, Kirsty, and her parents walked to their meeting place in the mall. "Knowing me, I'll fall flat on my face and totally embarrass myself."

"No, you won't," Kirsty reassured her, squeezing her hand. "You'll be fabulous. And everyone will love your rainbow jeans, I just know it."

Rachel smiled at her. "I'm so glad we're doing this together," she said.

"Me, too." Kirsty grinned. "All of our best adventures happen when we're together, don't they?"

The two girls exchanged a look, their eyes sparkling. No one else knew that they shared an amazing secret. They were friends with the fairies, and they had enjoyed lots of wonderful, magical fairy adventures. Sometimes, the girls had

even been turned into fairies themselves,
and had been able to fly!

This week, Kirsty was staying with
Rachel's family for fall break. Once again,
the two friends had found themselves
magically whisked away to Fairyland
when a brand-new fairy adventure began!
They'd been invited to see a fairy fashion
show, but it had unfortunately been
hijacked by Jack Frost. He and his
goblins had barged in, all wearing outfits
from Jack Frost's new designer label,
Ice Blue. Jack Frost had declared that
everyone should wear his line of clothes,
so they'd all look like him! Then, with a
crackling bolt of icy magic, he had stolen
the Fashion Fairies' seven magical objects
and vanished into the human world.

RAINBOW magic

These activities are magical!
Play dress-up, send friendship notes, and much more!

RAINBOW magic™

SPECIAL EDITION

Three Books in Each One—
More Rainbow Magic Fun!

Joy the Summer Vacation Fairy
Holly the Christmas Fairy
Kylie the Carnival Fairy
Stella the Star Fairy
Shannon the Ocean Fairy
Trixie the Halloween Fairy
Gabriella the Snow Kingdom Fairy
Juliet the Valentine Fairy
Mia the Bridesmaid Fairy
Flora the Dress-Up Fairy
Paige the Christmas Play Fairy
Emma the Easter Fairy
Cara the Camp Fairy
Destiny the Rock Star Fairy
Belle the Birthday Fairy
Olympia the Games Fairy
Selena the Sleepover Fairy
Cheryl the Christmas Tree Fairy
Florence the Friendship Fairy
Lindsay the Luck Fairy

■SCHOLASTIC

scholastic.com
rainbowmagiconline.com

HIT entertainment

RMSPECIAL10

RAINBOW magic ™

There's Magic in Every Series!

The Rainbow Fairies
The Weather Fairies
The Jewel Fairies
The Pet Fairies
The Fun Day Fairies
The Petal Fairies
The Dance Fairies
The Music Fairies
The Sports Fairies
The Party Fairies
The Ocean Fairies
The Night Fairies
The Magical Animal Fairies
The Princess Fairies
The Superstar Fairies

Read them all!

■SCHOLASTIC

scholastic.com
rainbowmagiconline.com

HiT entertainment

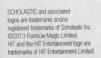
RMFAIRY7